When 10-year-old Ben Tennyson stumbles upon a mysterious alien device in the woods one summer, little does he realise that his life is set to change - forever.

As soon as the watch-like Omnitrix quite literally gets a grip on him, Ben discovers it gives him the ability to transform into 10 different alien super-beings, each one with awesome powers!

Using the Omnitrix to cause super-powered mischief turns out to be fun, but will Ben learn to use his might to fight for good?

READ ON AND FIND OUT . . .

EGMONT

We bring stories to life

Published in Great Britain 2009
by Egmont UK Limited
239 Kensington High Street, London W8 6SA

Ben 10 and all related characters and elements
are trademarks of and © Cartoon Network.
(s09)

Adapted from the animated series by
Barry Hutchison

1 3 5 7 9 10 8 6 4 2

A CIP catalogue record for this title is available from
the British Library

Printed and bound in Great Britain by the CPI Group

CHAPTER ONE

SIZE SOMETIMES MATTERS

Ben and Gwen stood in their swimming costumes, gazing up at the twisting tubes of the largest water slide either of them had ever seen.

'Six stories of twists and turns . . .' breathed Ben.

'Hurtling down a two-hundred-foot plunge . . .' continued Gwen.

'At speeds of over twenty-five miles per hour . . .'

They looked at each other and exchanged an excited high five. 'You've entered "The Riptide Rapids Zone",' they both cried.

Gwen was fastest off the mark. She dashed for the entrance to the slide with Ben in hot pursuit. This was going to be so awesome!

A hand appeared in front of Ben, forcing him to skid to a stop. A bored-looking pool attendant blocked his path. 'You're too short,' the attendant said.

'What are you talking about?' demanded Ben. The attendant pointed to a nearby height chart. It showed how tall a person had to be before they could ride the Riptide Rapids. Ben fell a few centimetres short. 'But I'm almost –'

'Next!'

Ben looked over at Gwen. Because she was a few centimetres taller than he was she'd been allowed through. Surely she'd help him, wouldn't she?

'Sorry. I heard the baby banana boats are fun for the smaller set,' Gwen chuckled before she skipped off to join the queue for the slide.

Ben snuck off behind the ticket booth, out of sight. He twisted the dial on the Omnitrix, searching for the right alien.

'They'll all feel small when Ripjaws shows up for a dip,' he muttered, slamming his hand down on the watch.

Nothing.

He raised his wrist and examined the device. The control dial seemed to be stuck. He pulled back his arm and whacked the watch against the ticket-booth wall.

That did it. With a **CRACK**, the dial snapped down into place and the familiar cloud of energy surrounded Ben, changing his DNA. Something felt different this time but, before he could figure out what it was, the change was complete.

He looked down at his tiny body, slapping his hand against his forehead in frustration. 'No, no, NO,' cried Grey Matter. 'Anything but being a micro munchkin!'

THUD-UM! THUD-UM! THUD-UM!

The ground beneath Grey Matter's feet began to shake. He staggered, trying to keep his balance. What was it? An earthquake? A landslide? He looked up and realised it was something even worse.

A gaggle of excited children was charging in his direction. They had their eyes fixed on the entrance to the water slide. Even if the kids did

look down and spot the miniature alien hero, they were going too fast to stop. They were going to squash him flat!

'Uh-oh,' Grey Matter gulped just before the mass of thundering feet surrounded him. He threw himself to one side, barely avoiding being crushed. A shadow passed over him and he sprang into a forwards roll, just as another foot slammed down where he had been.

'Whoa, look out!' he cried, weaving past another pair of legs. 'Watch those flip-flops.'

With a sigh of relief, Grey Matter dodged a final foot. He set off after the crowd of children, running as fast as his little legs would carry him. A customer was talking to the pool attendant, who was looking even more bored than usual.

This customer was a skinny man named Howell. He polished his glasses as he spoke. 'In nineteen fifty-one, when this water park was a cornfield, recently declassified documents suggest an alien spacecraft crash-landed right here,' he said.

With the attendant distracted, Grey Matter grabbed the chance to get his own back. He snuck over to where the men were talking and quickly knotted the attendant's shoelaces together.

'Time to tie up some loose ends,' he giggled quietly.

'So,' continued Howell, slipping his glasses back on, 'if you could get someone from upper management down here so I could start checking soil samples . . .'

'OK,' sighed the pool attendant. 'Hold on while I call someone who cares.' He placed a hand to his ear and pretended to dial a telephone number. 'Ring. Ring. Ring. Oh, guess what, dude?' he spat. 'No answer. Next in line!'

Howell sighed sadly and began to shuffle away. As he did, he spotted a tiny grey figure scampering up the steps towards the water slide.

'Did you just see that?' he spluttered. 'An alien! Maybe a remnant of that fateful crash.'

The attendant shook his head. 'Dude, you've been in the sun *way* too long.'

Dodging past him, Howell hurried after Grey Matter. The attendant moved to stop him but, as soon as he lifted a foot, his shoelaces pulled in opposite directions. With a **THUD** he crashed face first on to the ground.

Gwen was about to launch herself down

the slide when the little grey alien hopped up next to her. 'Hey, race you to the bottom,' he grinned, pushing himself off.

WHOOOOOOSH!

Grey Matter shot down the slide at blinding speed, flipping, twisting and turning all the way to the bottom. He flipped end over end in the air before landing in the pool with a very small **SPLASH**.

'Now that *rocked*,' he chirped, and then screamed as he realised Gwen was shooting from the end of the slide and hurtling towards him.

SPLAAAAASH!

Gwen's weight forced the tiny alien under. For a few frantic seconds he kicked and struggled until his head finally bobbed up above the surface of the water.

'Grandpa's not going to like you going alien just to sneak on a ride,' scolded Gwen.

Grey Matter shrugged. 'That's why I'm

not going to tell him. In a few minutes I'll be back to normal and he'll never know – *will* he?'

Shaking her head, Gwen began to wade over to the side of the pool. 'We gotta towel off,' she told him. 'Or in your case *napkin* off.'

Neither Gwen nor Grey Matter noticed the head rising out of the pool behind the little alien. Howell wiped the water from his glasses then reached out and snatched Grey Matter up in one hand.

'There you are,' he grinned. 'My little alien ticket to fame.'

'Gwen! Gwen!' cried Grey Matter as his captor hauled himself up out of the pool.

Gwen spun on the spot, recognising the panic in her cousin's voice. 'Let him go!' she cried as she realised what was happening.

Howell didn't listen. He snatched a lunch box from a picnic table and shoved Grey Matter into it. The alien yelped as he was bounced around inside.

Grandpa Max arrived at the poolside just as Howell barged past. He watched the man go, unaware that his grandson was being carried away.

'Grandpa, that guy's got Grey Matter!' shouted Gwen, already in hot pursuit of the fleeing kidnapper. Grandpa joined the chase, pushing his way through the crowds as he tried to keep up.

As they drew closer to the entrance of the water park, Grandpa stumbled to a stop. His legs ached and his lungs were burning from the effort of running. He couldn't take another step.

Gwen kept sprinting. Being smaller and younger, she was able to move through the crowds without too much trouble. In just a few seconds, she made it to the park entrance, leaping the turnstile in a single bound.

She skidded out into the car park – just in time to see a car speed by. The driver glanced at her as he accelerated past. Gwen saw the sunlight reflecting off the driver's glasses and knew she was too late.

Grey Matter had been taken. Her cousin was gone.

CHAPTER TWO

THE HOUSE THAT HOWELL BUILT

An automatic security camera tracked the car as it pulled into the garage of a large house. Howell got out, the lunch box tucked under his arm, and threw open the door leading through to the main building. A network of laser beams criss-crossed the hallway.

'Security system off,' he said. The beams fizzled away. 'Lights on. Prepare dinner.'

A row of lights along the ceiling blinked into life. Over in another part of the house, the microwave switched itself on. Howell barely paid any attention to these things as he hurried along the hallway. Behind him, two robotic vacuum cleaners cleaned up the soggy mess left by his wet feet.

A skinny grey cat hopped up on to the table just as the lunch box was set down. It sniffed at it and gave a hungry **MEOW**.

'No, no,' Howell scolded, pushing the cat to one side. 'This one is all mine.'

❉ ❉ ❉

The Rust Bucket sped along a city street, cutting its way through the mid-afternoon traffic. In the passenger seat, Gwen was trying to reassure herself everything would be OK.

'So, if he's Grey Matter now, he'll just turn back into Ben, then go Four Arms or something and escape,' she reasoned.

Grandpa wasn't so certain. 'But if he went alien when you said he did, Ben should've changed back before he was taken.'

'Which means maybe something's wrong

with the watch,' Gwen realised. 'Well,' she said hopefully, 'at least as Grey Matter he's smart.'

※ ※ ※

THWACK!

Grey Matter's head rebounded off the side of the glass jar he was now trapped in. It was the fifth time he'd tried the same escape technique and it was *really* starting to hurt.

Howell's face was so close it was almost pressed up against the glass. Behind the man, Grey Matter could make out statues, posters and action figures of one thing and one thing only: aliens.

'Incredible,' Howell whispered. 'Truly incredible. A perfect miniature alien being.'

'Who are you calling miniature?' demanded Grey Matter.

'So, which galaxy are you from?' quizzed Howell.

'Actually, I don't know myself,' admitted the tiny alien. 'And if I did I wouldn't tell you.'

'Ah, feisty little life form, aren't you?'

'You want to see feisty, just wait until I get big.' Grey Matter glared at Howell. The man just stared back, fascinated. 'Take a picture,' said Grey Matter, scowling, 'it'll last longer.'

Howell reached into his pocket and pulled out his mobile phone. He pointed the camera towards the figure inside the jar and snapped a photograph. 'My thoughts exactly.'

In the great hall of a grand old mansion house, an armoured man sat bathed in shadow. Enoch – leader of the Forever Knights – snarled behind his golden faceplate at an unwelcome sight on his communications-system monitor.

'Mr Howell,' he said, barely able to contain his displeasure, 'we've more than had enough of your fuzzy claims and blurry photos of supposed alien spaceships. I am not someone you want to annoy.'

'I know that,' replied Howell hurriedly. 'But this one's different, I promise you.' A close-up picture of Grey Matter appeared on Enoch's screen. 'See?' continued Howell. 'He's only about ten centimetres in size and converses fluently in English. Perhaps the Organisation would consider –'

'I'm sending a car,' said Enoch, interrupting him. On screen, Howell punched the air with delight. 'You better not be wasting our time,' Enoch warned. 'Or our resources.'

With a **CLICK**, he shut down the communication system. Behind his mask, he almost allowed himself a smile. Howell was an annoyance, but perhaps he was not completely useless after all.

❈ ❈ ❈

Grey Matter sat on the floor of his glass prison, his head resting on his hands. He could barely believe how unlucky he'd been.

'A thousand people at the water park and the UFO freak spots me,' he muttered.

MEEOW! Howell's cat hopped up on to the shelf where the jar was balanced. At first, Grey Matter pulled back in fright, but then an idea suddenly dawned on him.

'Wait . . . this could work,' he said. He rapped his knuckles on the glass and began to wave frantically at the cat. 'Here, kitty, kitty,' he called. 'I taste just like chicken.'

At that, the cat pounced, swiping at the jar with its front paws. Grey Matter braced for impact as the glass container toppled from the shelf and shattered on the carpet below.

'I'm free!' he cried, leaping to his feet. A sudden sucking sound caught his attention, making him turn. An automatic vacuum cleaner was speeding across the floor towards him on its way to clean up the broken glass. 'Uh-oh,' he gulped. 'I'm free.'

Grey Matter turned to run, only to find the cat blocking his escape. Its green eyes narrowed and it licked its lips as it closed in on what it hoped would be dinner.

Twisting away from the hungry feline, Grey Matter leaped over the approaching vacuum cleaner. A second machine was right behind it and he had to pull his legs up into a somersault to avoid being sucked inside.

Mistaking the alien for a large lump of dirt, the vacuums spun on the spot and began to give chase. Grey Matter scampered across the carpet and darted out into the hallway. He skidded round a corner, just as another door was pushed open.

'Howell Wainwright – alien discoverer,' beamed Howell, emerging into the hallway. He slipped his phone into his pocket and headed to his study to talk to his prize specimen again. 'Let the fame and fortune begin!'

A second later, his shriek of panic echoed around the house.

Meanwhile, Grey Matter had found his way into the kitchen. He darted for the nearest cupboards, all too aware that the vacuum cleaners were almost upon him. Springing upwards like a frog, the little alien latched on to a cupboard door handle and swung himself on to the kitchen worktop.

Down on the floor, the machines slowed

to a stop, no longer able to detect any dirt. Grey Matter sighed with relief; he was safe – for now. His eyes fell on a slim silver telephone that had been left on the kitchen worktop. He began pushing down the giant buttons. Maybe his luck was changing after all.

After a few rings, Gwen's voice crackled down the line. 'Hello?'

'Gwen, it's me.'

'Ben? You're still Grey Matter?'

'Yeah. The watch still won't work.'

'Where are you?'

Grey Matter dragged the handset across to the kitchen window and peered outside. 'There appears to be a mountain peak thirteen-point-two miles due west, with a vertical angle of forty-five degrees . . .'

'Brainiac,' Gwen snapped. 'How about a street?'

The alien peered at the buildings outside, searching for a street sign. 'Oh, yeah,' he said, leaning right up against the glass as he struggled to read a faraway notice, 'it's Ripley –'

AWOOGA! AWOOGA!

The very second that Grey Matter's hand pressed against the window an alarm began to wail. A flashing red light cast flickering shadows across the kitchen walls. Startled, the alien looked up, searching for a shut-off switch.

A shiver of terror travelled the length of Grey Matter's body. He couldn't see one anywhere – but he *could* see a metal security shutter sliding closed across the window. It moved quickly, slicing straight down towards the windowsill like a guillotine blade.

And straight towards his head!

CHAPTER THREE

FLUSHED

Kicking his feet against the glass, Grey Matter propelled himself backwards. The shutter slammed down a split-second later, narrowly missing the alien hero's legs.

Stumbling, Grey Matter bumped into the telephone. He heard Gwen's voice calling to him as the handset toppled from the kitchen worktop. With a **CRACK** the plastic casing shattered on the floor.

As he gazed down at the smashed telephone, a pair of feet stepped through the mess of broken plastic. Grey Matter looked up into the determined eyes of Howell.

Rushing forwards, Howell brought both

hands down over the alien, pinning him against the worktop. For a moment he thought he'd won, until the tiny grey shape scrabbled up his arm and inside his sleeve.

Howell squirmed as Grey Matter scampered around inside his shirt. He slapped at the bump moving over his chest and missed. Again and again Howell slapped himself, desperately trying to catch the wriggling little alien.

Finally, with a spectacular leap, Grey Matter hurled himself through the neck of Howell's shirt. The man threw out his arms to catch him, missed, and toppled to the floor with a *THUD*.

Moving quickly, Grey Matter bolted for an air vent in the wall and squeezed himself through it. Almost at once, the metal grate was torn from the wall and a hand was thrust inside.

Strong fingers wrapped around the alien's frail body and began to drag him out.

There was only one thing for it.

'Owww!' yelped Howell as Grey Matter bit down hard on his thumb. The tiny hero hopped free and hurried deeper into the air-conditioning system. He may have escaped for the moment, but he wasn't out of danger yet.

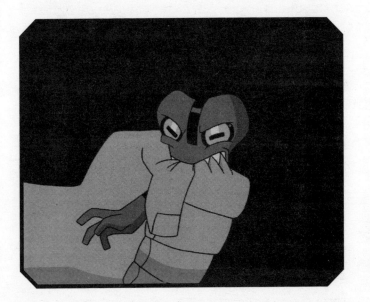

❈ ❈ ❈

In The Rust Bucket, Gwen was studying a road map, searching for the street her cousin had been trying to tell her about. It wasn't proving easy.

'Ripley Avenue, Ripley Lane, Ripley Drive,' she read. 'We don't have time to check them all out.'

Grandpa Max dropped down a gear and floored the accelerator. His face was grim and his tone was serious. 'Do we have a choice?'

❈ ❈ ❈

In the darkness of the air-conditioning system, Grey Matter heaved himself up another narrow shaft. He had no idea where he was going, but he hoped whatever was up ahead was safer than what he'd left behind.

'What's your malfunction?' he snapped, talking out loud to the Omnitrix. 'Probably something stupid, like the DNA splicing replicator copying a fragmented amino acid sequence.'

He stopped, amazed at his thoughts. 'So *this* is what it feels like to be smart,' he wondered.

Suddenly, an icy wind whipped around him, chilling him to the bone. The little alien tried to keep moving, but the wind quickly increased in strength. It stung his eyes and took his breath away.

'I'll teach you to blow me off,' bellowed Howell from somewhere not too far away. Grey Matter gulped. Howell had switched on the air conditioning!

A fierce gust hit the alien hard. He fought to hold on, but the wind was now too powerful. With a wail of terror, Grey Matter found himself spinning and bouncing helplessly through the inner workings of the air-conditioning system.

CRUNCH! His back was driven hard against the metal wall of the vent.

CRACK! His shoulder smashed painfully against a raised edge.

BADOOM! The shaft shook as his head thudded off a temperature regulator.

Finally, Grey Matter's fingers snared on another metal vent and he came to an abrupt stop. Through the narrow gaps he could see he was at ceiling level, looking down on an empty room below. It was a long way to fall, but it would be better than being thrown around inside the shafts.

The metal grate swung downwards as Grey Matter unclipped the latch. His stomach lurched and for a moment he thought he was going to fall, but he managed to cling on. He hung there for a moment, dangling from the vent and breathing a sigh of relief.

'Gotcha!'

Howell charged into the room, swinging a broom as if it were a sword. Grey Matter threw himself from the vent just in the nick of time.

'Think again!' cried the little alien, flipping over Howell's head and bolting out of the room.

He found himself back in the kitchen. Behind him, Howell was already giving chase. The windows were all closed and there were no other doors. Grey Matter's brilliant brain raced. There had to be another way out. There *had* to be.

Ah-ha!

Bounding up on to the worktops, he began a mad dash for the sink. Howell's shadow loomed above him and Grey Matter launched himself into a desperate slide. This was going to be close!

Howell's hands came down just as the alien slid into the sink and down the plughole. The man cried out in frustration as he saw his prize specimen slip through his fingers yet again.

'He gets away and the Organisation will

come after me,' fretted Howell.

His eyes fell to the tap. Just inside the drainage pipe, Grey Matter braced himself for what he knew was coming next.

WHOOSH!

A torrent of water gushed into the sink and swirled down the plughole. Grey Matter barely had time to take one big deep breath before the tide swept him swiftly through the plumbing system.

His tiny lungs burned as he struggled against the flow of water. For a moment it was like being back on the Riptide Rapids slide, only darker, scarier and much more dangerous.

A narrower pipe split off from the one he was zooming along and he somehow managed to swim into it. The water was calmer in here and he was able to move along it quickly. He could see light up above and he kicked harder, fighting to reach the surface before the last of his air ran out.

With a gasp, his head broke the surface of the water. He breathed in deeply, filling his lungs with precious oxygen.

'Ahh! Fresh air!' he panted.

He relaxed a little and studied his surroundings. Only then did he realise that he was bobbing up and down in Howell's toilet.

'This,' he muttered, 'is *so* gross.'

※ ※ ※

The Rust Bucket pulled up at the first place on the map – Ripley Avenue. Gwen and Grandpa hopped down and studied the neat rows of houses.

'I'll take this side, you take that one,' said Gwen. Grandpa nodded and set off to check his side of the street. If Ben were here, they'd find him.

Somehow.

✖ ✖ ✖

Howell sat at the desk in his computer room, watching a dozen monitors. They each showed an image of a different part of the house. It was times like these that it paid to have the best security system money could buy.

'You can run, but you can't hide,' he chortled, his eyes flicking from screen to screen. He adjusted the zoom control of one camera and a wicked smile spread across his lips. The alien was in the basement, standing on top of an electrical control box and . . . waving!

Howell watched in horror as Grey Matter yanked the control box open and flicked a switch. At once, every one of his twelve monitor screens became black and the room was plunged into darkness.

Furious, Howell leaped up from the desk and rushed down to the basement, taking the stairs three at a time. He burst through the door in time to see Grey Matter scurry up the chimney.

Howell's fingers fumbled in his pocket until he found what he was looking for: he pulled out a box of matches and rushed to the fireplace.

'I'll smoke you out if I have to!' he cried, striking a match against the side of the box. It spluttered into life and he let it fall amongst the logs and coal in the grate. With a **CRACKLE** the flames took hold and clouds of choking black smoke began to billow up the chimney.

CHAPTER FOUR

THE HAND OVER

Grey Matter could see daylight far above him. He climbed quickly up the brickwork of the chimney, closer and closer to the safety of the outside world.

Suddenly, he felt a burst of heat below him. He looked down to see the thick smoke cloud approaching. When he looked up again, the distant circle of daylight had been completely blotted out.

Blinded by the grey-black fog, Grey Matter began to cough. The chimney was narrow and the smoke swirled all around him, making him lightheaded and his arms weak.

Eventually, his fingers lost their grip and

he plummeted down towards the flickering flames in the fireplace.

SWISH!

A butterfly net swept up to meet him, catching him before he landed in the fire. He didn't know whether to cheer or cry. On the one hand, he had narrowly escaped being cooked, but on the other hand there was no escaping the fact that he had been well and truly caught.

✖ ✖ ✖

The Rust Bucket cornered sharply on to another street. This was the third one they'd tried and so far Ben was nowhere to be seen.

Gwen's eyes suddenly grew wide with surprise. She pointed towards a garage where the back end of a familiar vehicle could just be seen.

'Grandpa!' she shouted. 'His car!'

The glass door of a large display case closed firmly behind Grey Matter. Howell turned the key in the lock. He was taking no chances this time.

Grey Matter looked out at the room. Several more display cases lined the walls. They contained models and toys from some *very*

geeky sci-fi movies and TV shows.

'Something tells me you're the type of guy who has a lot of friends,' he said sarcastically.

'Who needs friends when you have the fame I'm about to experience?' replied Howell, his eyes blazing with excitement. From outside the house the pair heard a screech of tyres. 'They're here,' said Howell nervously.

'Yeah. To break me out.'

The door creaked open and Grey Matter gasped. The three men marching into the room were *not* there to rescue him. As if their gleaming metal faceplates hadn't been warning enough, the box the first man carried was a dead giveaway. It buzzed scarily with electrical energy. Grey Matter knew it must be a prison, and there was only one person small enough to fit inside: him!

'Where is the alien?' demanded the knight with the box.

Howell glanced at the display cabinet. It

was all the information the knight needed. With a sharp elbow he knocked Howell to one side, then smashed through the display cabinet's glass with an ironclad fist.

'Hands off!' protested Grey Matter, but the Forever Knight had no intention of letting go. He dropped the squirming alien inside the energy prison and sealed it shut.

❈ ❈ ❈

'Wanna ring the doorbell?' asked Gwen as she and her grandfather hurried up a garden path.

Grandpa Max raised his foot. 'I'll knock. Hard.'

KER-ACK!

The door splintered off its hinges and Grandpa hurried along the hallway, reaching the end just as a startled old lady trundled out of the kitchen in her wheelchair.

For a moment, Grandpa and the woman

just looked at each other, neither one quite sure how to react. It was the old lady who finally broke the silence.

'Brutus,' she growled. 'Sic, boy.'

A snarling ball of fur and teeth bounded from the kitchen and launched itself at Grandpa Max. He managed to catch the dog by the neck,

but it thrashed around wildly, snapping at him with its powerful jaws. Struggling against the brute, Grandpa staggered into the garden, tripped on the step and fell backwards on to the path.

Meanwhile, Gwen had spotted some suspicious goings on at the next house. Three masked men came out of the front door and began climbing into a long black car. One of them carried a box, while the other two dragged another man between them. As the man struggled, his mobile phone toppled from his pocket and bounced into the grass.

'It's him,' said Gwen, 'the guy who's got Ben!'

Grandpa had just about had enough of the dog. His grandson was in trouble and he didn't have time to wrestle with the mutt.

'Down, boy,' he said in a low voice. He gave the dog a tap on the head, just behind one of its ears. Instantly, the animal's eyes glazed over and the savage expression vanished from its face.

'Nice trick, Grandpa,' said Gwen as her grandfather gently set the unconscious dog down on the path.

The car screeched round a corner at the end of the street and zoomed off out of sight. It was moving too fast. They'd never be able to catch up.

'Come on, we need to find out where they went,' barked Grandpa Max, rushing over to check out the house the men had appeared from. There had to be a clue. There *had* to be, otherwise there was a very good chance they'd never see Ben again.

❋ ❋ ❋

Grey Matter stumbled around inside the energy prison as the car sped along an uneven driveway. The box was wedged between Howell and one of the knights. The other two knights sat in front, silent behind their masks.

'I have a bad feeling about these guys,' said Grey Matter.

Howell smirked. 'That's because you're the one in the cage and I'm not.'

The car's tyres crunched noisily on the gravel driveway and the vehicle came to a sharp stop. Howell's door was pulled open and another Forever Knight yanked him out. The knight on the back seat snatched up the energy prison and climbed out to join the others. One by one, they filed in through the front door of a large mansion.

❈ ❈ ❈

Back at Howell's, Gwen had found the mobile phone the kidnapper had dropped. A close-up photograph of Grey Matter was still on its screen.

'He looks so sad,' she said. A sudden wave of anger rushed over her. 'They can't torment Ben like that. Only *I* can torment Ben like that.'

Grandpa Max prised the phone from her clenched hand and checked the call history. The last number had been dialled less than an hour ago. 'If we can get a reverse trace on that number, we should be able to get an address,' he said.

Gwen smiled. 'Grandpa, there's a sneaky side to you I'm totally starting to appreciate.'

❈ ❈ ❈

Inside the grand hall of the mansion, a Forever Knight set the energy prison down on a table. Across the table, Enoch leaned forwards.

'A remarkable specimen,' he said.

Howell hopped from one foot to the other, barely able to contain his glee. 'So, how are we doing this?' he babbled. 'Joint news conference, hitting the major talk shows . . .?'

'We prefer to keep our discoveries private,' snapped Enoch.

Howell's face fell. 'What are you talking about? We have to tell the world about this.'

Enoch motioned towards a group of sinister-looking scientists. Each one wore a long white coat and a black hood covered his head. 'Actually, we don't.'

The scientists pushed past Howell and lifted the box from the table. Howell could only watch as they walked off with the alien.

'Where are you taking him?'

'Our scientists have a few . . . *tests* to run.'

'I found him!' cried Howell. 'He belongs to me.'

'He's ours now,' said Enoch, his voice low and threatening. 'And *you* just became disposable.'

✳ ✳ ✳

Howell tucked in his chin and pulled his hands over his head, trying to protect himself as he bounced and rolled down a flight of solid stone steps. The wind was knocked from his body when he slammed against the final step and down on to the chilly slate floor.

At the head of the stairs, two Forever Knights watched him pull himself up and limp towards the exit. When he was out of sight, however, Howell doubled back and made for another door that led deeper into the mansion.

'They can't do this,' he mumbled to himself. 'To either of us.'

Howell rolled up his sleeves and gritted his teeth. One way or another, he was getting his alien back.

CHAPTER FIVE

AN EXPLOSIVE ENCOUNTER

*O*utside the mansion, Gwen and Grandpa clambered up the branches of a tall tree. In the grounds below, six or seven knights stood guard.

'This isn't a house, it's a fortress,' Gwen whispered.

'They call themselves the Organisation,' Grandpa replied quietly. 'A well-financed secret society dedicated to collecting alien technology.'

They both looked down at the branch they were standing on. It was long and thick and led almost all the way to one of the mansion's many balconies. Making the jump would be risky, but it was the only way they could get inside.

'Ready?' asked Grandpa Max.

Gwen took a deep breath. 'Not really, but . . .' She nodded and, with that, they began to run.

✖ ✖ ✖

The energy prison sat on a narrow table in a high-tech operating theatre. Grey Matter's eyes were fixed on the operating table, where a cardboard model of him was strapped in place.

BZZZZZZT!

A pencil-thin laser beam spat from a gun-shaped piece of machinery. The beam quickly sliced the cardboard model to pieces – legs first, then arms and head.

One of the scientists nodded, satisfied that the equipment was working properly. He turned and nodded to his lab partner. 'Prepare the subject for dissection.'

Gwen and Grandpa launched themselves from the branch as fast and as far as they could. For a moment, Gwen felt like she was hanging in the air and then suddenly she was falling towards the ground.

THUD!

Her flailing arms found the edge of the balcony and she swung hard against the rough stone wall. Beside her, Grandpa Max had already begun to heave himself up. Gwen kicked her feet against the brickwork and grandfather and granddaughter tumbled over the balcony into a long narrow corridor.

They had made it inside. The hard part was done.

Now came the *really* hard part: finding Ben.

✕ ✕ ✕

In the lab, Grey Matter had been strapped to the table. He wriggled and fought, but the metal bonds holding him in place were too tight.

'Don't bother with the slice and dice,' he yelped as one of the scientists adjusted the settings on the laser. 'Trust me, I'm just as grey on the inside as I am on the outside.'

The door to the lab slid open and another scientist entered. His hood muffled his voice, but Grey Matter couldn't help but think it was somehow familiar.

'Let me assist you,' he told his colleague, stepping closer. With a sudden jerk, the new arrival smashed a fire extinguisher against the side of the scientist's head, sending him sprawling to the floor.

Howell pulled off his hood and slipped on his glasses. He adjusted the settings on the slicing machine and took careful aim.

'What are you doing?' gasped Grey Matter.

'Getting you out of here!'

Grey Matter felt the heat of the lasers as they sliced through the metal restraints. He hopped up on to the table, free at last.

Several other scientists flooded into the room. They dived for Grey Matter, but Howell hurled himself at them, fists flying. 'Back off,' he warned. 'Aliens are people too!'

Grey Matter darted out into the corridor,

only to crash into someone's leg. He looked up
to see Gwen looking down at him.

'Ben!'

'Gwen!'

Gwen picked her tiny cousin up. Grandpa
rested a hand on her shoulder and steered her
through a door just as a squadron of knights
clanked past and an alarm began to sound.

'Let's save the family reunion for the
road,' he suggested.

The room they had entered was dark, but as they stepped through the door a series of overhead lights clicked on. All three of them gave a gasp of surprise as they saw what they had stumbled upon.

Fifty or more display tables filled the room, each one containing a different piece of futuristic-looking equipment. Grey Matter's eyes grew wide with wonder.

'Look at all this alien tech,' he said. 'These guys have no clue what they've got here.'

'Or maybe they do,' said Gwen.

'We've got to destroy everything,' announced Grey Matter. This type of technology was too dangerous for the knights to have.

Before the heroes could act, another door slid open on the far side of the room. Enoch and a platoon of his knights entered, dragging a struggling Howell with them.

'Spread out and find them,' ordered Enoch.

Grandpa and Gwen ducked out of sight behind a large alien machine. Grey Matter's eyes scanned the objects on either side and a plan began to form in his super-intelligent alien brain.

'Gwen, grab that pulse hypercore,' he whispered, pointing to one of the items. He hopped on to the closest table and pointed to another. 'Grandpa, the gallenium capacitor.'

Gwen peered at him, not quite sure if he was being serious or not.

'It's not Ben talking, it's Grey Matter!' insisted the alien. 'Do it.'

Grandpa and Gwen darted over and collected the items. As they sat them on the table, a laser blast scorched the air beside them.

'They're over here!' cried one of the knights.

'Get out of here,' urged Grey Matter as he heaved the smaller items over to the large one. 'If I can get inside the power grid, I can hook the hypercore and capacitor up to it. This is where small comes in handy. No, go! I'll meet you outside.'

Another blast exploded close to Gwen's head. Grandpa threw an arm round her shoulders and together they dodged and ducked between the objects until they finally made it to the exit.

Inside the large alien machine, Grey Matter was already hard at work. He twisted cables and slotted pieces together until the machine began to hum with power.

As Enoch approached the device, he realised what was about to happen. 'That reaction will decimate the mansion and everything in it. Everyone out!' he commanded urgently. Spinning on his heels, he caught Howell roughly by the front of his coat. 'Except you. You and your little alien have been nothing but trouble.'

He threw Howell to the ground and hurried after his fleeing knights, a split second before Grey Matter began to clamber from within the machine.

BLEEP!

A bright red flash made Howell look up. A boy was standing by the machine looking surprised but relieved.

'Huh? Where'd you come from?'

'I'll tell you later,' said Ben. 'But right now we gotta get outta here!'

A few minutes later, Grandpa, Gwen, Ben and Howell stood in the mansion grounds watching a series of explosions tear the place apart. Ben allowed himself a smile. There would be no way any of the alien gadgets could survive this.

'Anyone see where that little alien went?' asked Howell.

Ben did his best to look innocent. 'Nope.'

'Not a clue,' added Gwen.

Howell shook his head and began to march off down the driveway. 'Well,' he said with a sigh, 'I am *done* with anything alien!'

Ben watched him go, then turned and followed Grandpa and Gwen towards The Rust Bucket. 'It feels good to be big again,' he said.

'"Big"?' snorted Gwen. 'Get real, shorty.'

'Don't make me go Four Arms on you,' warned Ben.

Inside The Rust Bucket, Grandpa grinned, listening to his grandchildren bickering. It had been a close-run thing for a while, but it was safe to say that everything was back to normal.

At least, for now.

BEN 10 BOOK COLLECTION

HAVE YOU SEEN THEM ALL?

Ben 10 Alien Force Annual 2010	978 1 4052 4653 8; £7.99
Ben 10 Alien Force colour storybook 1 (Ben 10 Returns Part 1/Part 2)	978 1 4052 4799 3; £4.99
Ben 10 Alien Force colour storybook 2 (The Gauntlet/Be-Knighted)	978 1 4052 4800 6; £4.99
Ben 10 Amazing 3D Hero Vision	978 1 4052 4413 8; £3.99
Ben 10 Puzzle and Quiz Book	978 1 4052 4492 3; £3.99
Ben 10 Magnet Book	978 1 4052 4599 9; £5.99
Ben 10 All Action Stories & Flicker Book	978 1 4052 4512 8; £4.99
Ben 10 comic book 1 (And Then There Were 10)	978 1 4052 4663 7; £4.99
Ben 10 comic book 2 (Washington B.C.)	978 1 4052 4664 4; £4.99
Ben 10 comic book 3 (The Krakken)	978 1 4052 4804 4; £4.99

Ben 10 comic book 4	
(Permanent Retirement)	978 1 4052 4805 1; £4.99
Ben 10 chapter storybook 1	
(And Then There Were 10/Kevin 11)	978 1 4052 4467 1; £3.99
Ben 10 chapter storybook 2	
(The Alliance/Secrets)	978 1 4052 4468 8; £3.99
Ben 10 chapter storybook 3	
(Truth/Framed)	978 1 4052 4672 9; £4.99
Ben 10 chapter storybook 4	
(The Galactic Enforcers/Ultimate Weapon) 978 1 4052 4673 6; £4.99	

Visit Egmont.co.uk